MINECRAFT

◼MOJANG

Special thanks to Alex Wiltshire, Jennifer Hammervald,
Filip Thoms, Amanda Ström, and Isabella Balk

Published in the United States by Random House Children's Books, a division of
Penguin Random House LLC, 1745 Broadway, New York, NY 10019, and in Canada by
Penguin Random House Limited, Toronto. Random House and the colophon are
registered trademarks of Penguin Random House LLC.

First published in Great Britain 2019 by Egmont Books UK Ltd 2 Minster Court, 10th
floor, London EC3R 7BB.

rhcbooks.com
minecraft.net

ISBN 978-0-593-37937-0 (pbk.) | ISBN 978-0-593-37938-7 (ebook)

Printed in the United States of America

10 9 8 7 6 5 4 3 2 1

MOJANG
MINECRAFT

By Dan Morgan
Illustrated by Joe McLaren

Random House 🏠 New York

IN THE BEGINNING . . .

As always, we begin in the Overworld.
Get ready to giggle!

Q How do trees get on the internet?

A They log on.

Q Did you hear about the mountains that told jokes?

A They were "hill areas."

Do you like the lakes in the Overworld?

Q Why is grass dangerous?

A Because it's full of blades.

Q How many trees did Steve chop down?

A How wood I know?

They really float my boat!

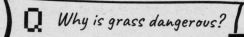

ZOMBIE ZINGERS

Try not to laugh your head off reading these gruesome gags.

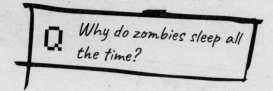

Q Why do zombies sleep all the time?

A Because they're dead tired.

Q How do you stop a zombie from attacking?

A You block its path.

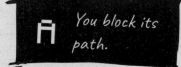

DIE LAUGHING

Don't laugh so much you have to respawn!

Q Did you hear about the zombie that was brilliant at attacks?

A He was very dead-icated.

Q What did the zombie say when it met Steve?

A Pleased to eat you.

Q What was the baby zombie's favorite toy?

A Its dead-y bear.

Q Why did the chicken jockey cross the road?

A To get to the other side.

Q What's a zombie's favorite bean?

A A human bean.

Q Why did the zombie go to the doctor?

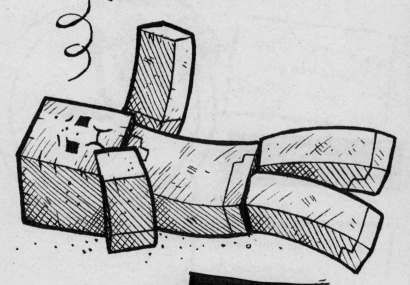

A It was feeling green.

JOKE JOURNEY

Let's hope these puns don't go south!

Q Why did Alex sit on the clock?

A She wanted to be on time.

Q Why did Steve take iron and gold in his boat?

A He needed oars.

Q Did you hear about the hungry clock?

A It went back four seconds.

Alex: OK, I've found north, south, and east on the compass.

Steve: Where's the west of it?

Steve: I was going to tell a compass joke but I've lost my bearings.

Alex: I wrote a joke about a broken compass but I'm not sure where I'm going with it.

13

RIDICULOUS REDSTONE

A hearty chuckle is just a stone's throw away.

Q What is redstone ore used for?

A Rowing a redstone boat.

Steve: I'd tell you the joke about the redstone circuit, but I'd just be repeating myself.

Q What did Steve say to the sad redstone lamp?

A Lighten up!

Q Why does Alex love redstone lamps?

A *Because they light up her life.*

Q Why don't llamas like redstone dust up their nose?

A Well, would you like it?

PLEASED TO EAT YOU

Sink your teeth into these meaty morsels.

Q How do you know when your mutton has gone rotten?

A It tastes baaaaad!

Q What do sheep wear to keep their hooves warm in winter?

A Woolly muttons.

Q What's a pig's favorite karate move?

A A pork chop.

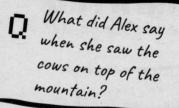

Q What did Alex say when she saw the cows on top of the mountain?

A The steaks have never been higher.

Steve: Did I sleep through dinner?

Alex: Yes, big "missed steak."

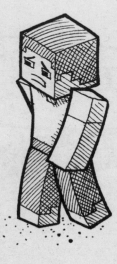

HORSING AROUND

We think mule find these jokes a-NEIGH-zing!

Q *Where do you take a sick horse?*

A *To the horse-pital.*

Q *What do you call a donkey with 3 legs?*

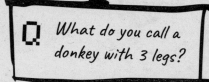

A *A wonky.*

Q *What do you call a donkey with 4 legs?*

A *Stable.*

Q Did you hear about the mule who had a sore throat?

A She was a little hoarse.

Q Did you hear about the mule that lived next to the horse?

A They were neigh-bors.

A *A night-mare.*

JOB JOKES

Who says having a job can't be fun?

Q *Why did the cow jump over the moon?*

A *Steve had cold hands when he was milking it.*

Q *What do librarians wear on their feet?*

A *Shhhhhhoes.*

Q Why are blacksmiths so interesting?

A They're always riveting.

Q Why are blacksmiths ahead of their time?

A They were shaping metal before it was cool.

Q What do you call someone who steals from the butcher?

A A hamburglar.

TICKLE YOUR FUNNY BONE

These skeleton jokes will hit you in the right spot.

Q Did you hear about the skeleton who used his bow and arrow in the dark?

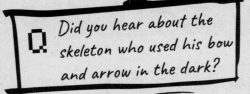

A He didn't know what he was missing.

Q What do you call a skeleton who can't be bothered to attack?

A Lazy bones.

Q What do you call a skeleton who stays in the snowy tundra too long?

A A numbskull.

Q Did you hear about the skeleton who broke another skeleton's bow and arrow?

A Now they're arch(er) enemies.

Q Why are skeletons good at telling jokes?

A Because they're so humerus.

GRUESOME GAGS

More jokes to really make you scream with laughter!

Q Why do skeletons hate being high up in the mountains?

A The cold goes right through them.

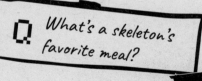

Q What's a skeleton's favorite meal?

A Spare ribs.

Q What instrument do skeletons play?

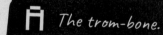

A The trom-bone.

Q How does a skeleton make you laugh?

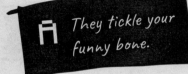

A They tickle your funny bone.

Q Why do skeletons get scared easily?

A They have no guts.

FISHY FUNNIES

This is dolphin-ately the plaice for some fin-tastic fish jokes.

Q *What party game do fish play?*

A *Salmon Says.*

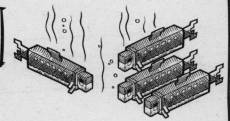

Q *What do you call a fish with no eyes?*

A *A fsh.*

Alex: Do dolphins do things by accident?

Steve: No, they're on porpoise.

Q What kind of photos do turtles take?

A Shellfies.

Q What do you do on a turtle's birthday?

A Shellebrate!

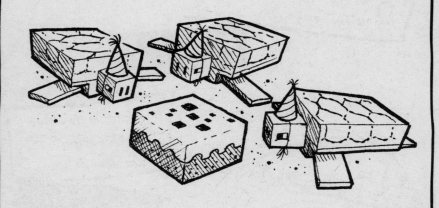

Two fish were swimming when it started raining. One said to the other, "Quick, get under the bridge. We're going to get wet!"

A TOOLBOX OF TITTERS

Don't be a spanner—let yourself be tickled by these tool jokes.

Q Did you hear that Alex got hit by a pickaxe?

A Don't worry, she only suffered miner injuries.

Alex: I've invented the shovel.

Steve: Sounds ground-breaking.

Q What do you call a man with a shovel?

A Doug.

Q So what do you call him when he's lost it?

A Douglas.

Q Did you hear about the artist who could make anything using shears?

A She was a shear genius.

Q What happened when the lumberjack hit the creeper?

A It axe-ploded.

THESE JOKES ROCK!

Put yourself between a rock and a funny place.

Q What did Alex say to the diamond ore?

A I dig you.

Q What did the diamond say to the coal?

A I've been under a lot of pressure recently.

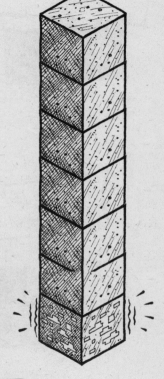

Q What music do ore blocks listen to?

A Rock music.

Q *Did you hear about the mining accident?*

A *It was ore-ful.*

Steve: Did you hear about the villager who hated coal?

Alex: No.

Steve: Never mined.

Alex: What's your favorite ore? Emerald or lapis lazuli?

Steve: Either ore.

ORE-SOME JOKES

Have a giggle at these gems.

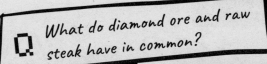

Q What do diamond ore and raw steak have in common?

A They're both rare.

Q What do you see when you look underneath some ore?

A Rock bottom.

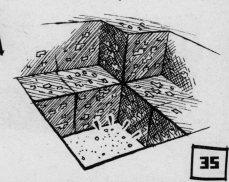

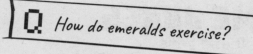

Q How do emeralds exercise?

A Gemnastics.

Q Why did the Nether quartz ore quit?

A Everyone took it for granite.

Q How did Alex get extra ore?

A With good fortune.

ORE-FULLY FUNNY

Roar along with these ore-fully good jokes.

Q *What did the ore block say to the miner?*

A *Pick me!*

Q Why is redstone messy?

A Because of all the dust.

Q When were redstone jokes the funniest?

A During the Stone Age.

Q Why are iron ingot-makers always accused of being gassy?

A Because whoever smelt it dealt it.

Q What do gold ore and farts have in common?

A They both smelt.

WATER LOTTA LAUGHS

Cry tears of laughter as you read these witty, watery wisecracks.

Q What should you collect icy water in?

A A cold-ron.

Q Why did the fish blush?

A Because it saw the ocean's bottom.

Q Where do the drowned like to swim?

A The Dead Sea.

Q What reminder did Steve write when he needed infinite water?

A Get well soon.

CROP TO IT!

Plant a smile on your face and let these jokes grow on you.

Q Did you hear about the chicken that ate all the seeds?

A It still felt peck-ish.

Q Why did the chicken stay at home?

A Because it felt fowl.

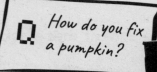

Q How do you fix a pumpkin?

A With a pumpkin patch.

Q Did you hear about the sickly carrot?

A It wasn't peeling very well.

Q What do you call it when a pig rolls over a potato?

A Mashed pork-tato.

Q Why won't crops grow in the Nether?

A Because they wither away.

45

MINE MANIA

You'll need to dig deep for these belly laughs.

Q. Why couldn't Steve get to the emerald ore?

A. Something was blocking his way.

Q. Where do tired miners sleep?

A. On bedrock.

EXPLOSIVE LAUGHS

These jokes will really creep up on you!

Q What is a creeper's favorite subject at school?

A Hisssssstory!

sssssSSSSSSSSSSSS

Q What do Australian creepers use to hunt?

A BOOMerangs.

Q Did you hear about the creeper's birthday party?

A It really went off with a BANG!

Q Why aren't creepers good in arguments?

A They have a short fuse.

Q Why did the creeper cross the road?

A To get to the other sssssside.

BOOM BOOM!

Get ready to explode with laughter!

Q Why are creepers prone to jealousy?

A Because they're green with envy.

Q What happened when Alex noticed the creeper was following her?

A It blew its opportunity.

Q What do creepers play their music on?

A A BOOMbox.

Q Why do creepers love going to parties?

A Because they always have a blast.

Q Why was the creeper excited when it got hit by lightning?

A It was all charged up.

INTO THE NETHER

Get ready for some fiery fun!

Q Did you hear about the skeleton that found romance in the Nether?

A He fell head over heels in lava.

Steve: I'm struggling to think of a lava joke.

Alex: You should just let it flow.

Q What did Alex say after she escaped the Nether?

A Nether again.

Q What did Alex say when she returned to the Nether?

A Never say Nether.

A Sole sand.

Q How did Steve feel when he saw that his Nether portal had been destroyed?

A A-ghast.

NETHER AGAIN

Spending time in the Nether is a real scream!

Q Why can't you get a good night's sleep in the Nether?

A Because the beds explode.

Steve: I tried bringing water into the Nether.

Alex: Big mist-take.

Q Why was the zombie pigman tired?

A Because he was dead on his feet.

Q Did you hear about the snow golem that spawned in the Nether?

A It had a meltdown.

Q Why was the zombie pigman late?

A Because he was a slow pork.

GOLEM GAGS

Make snow mistake, these jokes are ironclad.

Q Why can't snow golems play football?

A Snowballs allowed.

Q What did the fire say when it met the snow golem?

A Pleased to melt you.

Q What did the iron golem give to the villager's grandfather?

A grand poppy.

Q What do you call a golem that's not there?

A Snow golem.

Q Did you hear about the iron golem that fell in water?

A It got that sinking feeling.

61

PLANT PUNS AND FLOWER FUNNIES

These jokes are blooming hilarious.

Q What did the flower say when it had a little accident?

A I wet my plants!

Q Did you hear about the panda that lost its bamboo?

A It was bamboo-zled.

Q Did you see the cactus in the tuxedo?

A It was looking sharp.

Q Which flower grows right under your nose?

A Tulips.

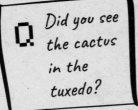

Q What do trees put on before swimming?

A Their trunks.

WITTY WEAPONS

Let's hope you get the point with these puns.

Q What did the axe say when it was in a hurry?

A Chop-chop!

Q What did Alex say when Steve held the sword upside down?

A That's not the point.

Q. Why are drowned mobs great at throwing tridents?

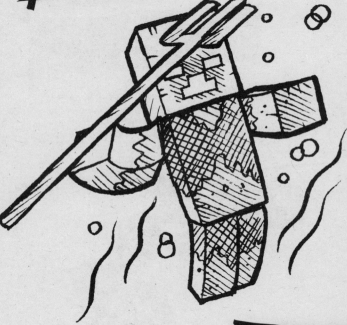

A. Because they always aim high.

Q *Have you heard about the enthusiastic sword?*

A *It always takes a stab at everything.*

Q *Have you heard about the broken sword?*

A *It's pointless.*

LOOKS LIKE BAD WITHER

Here are some more jokes, wither or not you want them!

Q Why is the wither always itchy?

A It has soul sand all over its body.

Q Why are the wither's plans so good?

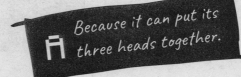

A Because it can put its three heads together.

Q Why is the wither still single?

A Because it's immune to lava.

Q What do you call the wither in winter?

A A bunch of numbskulls.

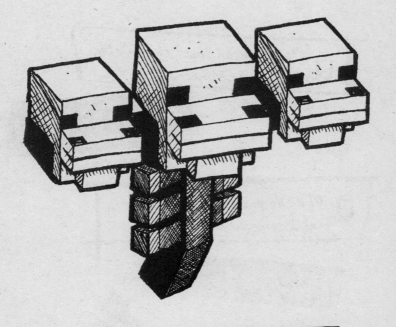

Q *What do you get when you cross a wither with a chicken?*

A *Fowl wither.*

CRAFTY CHUCKLES

Let your laughter build and build.

Q Did you hear about the painter who played Minecraft?

A She was good at arts and crafts.

Q What do you call it when a witch makes something?

A Witchcraft.

Steve: My recipe book fell on my head.

Alex: That must have hurt.

Steve: Well, I've only got my shelf to blame.

Q What did one wall say to the other wall?

A Meet you at the corner.

Q Did you hear Steve had too many books?

A He never did have any shelf control.

SLEEP ON THESE

These jokes are simply dreamy!

Q Why can't you trust someone sleeping in a bed?

A Because they're lying.

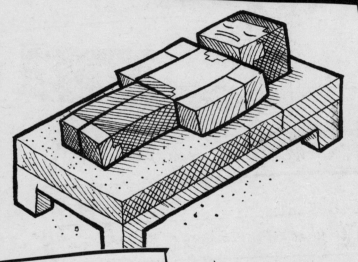

Q Did you hear about the miner who had trouble nodding off?

A He had to rock himself to sleep.

Q Did you hear about the naughty miner who didn't want to sleep?

A He was resisting a rest.

73

Q Why did Alex stop brewing?

A She lost her bottle.

Q What do you call a cauldron once it's warmed up?

A A hot-ron.

Q Why is brewing an enlightening experience?

A Because of all the glowstone dust.

When Alex saw Steve struggling to make a potion, she knew there was trouble brewing.

Q Did you hear about the player who threw all his potions?

A He really caused a splash.

JUST WING IT

A little bird told us you like eggs-cellent jokes.

Q What do you get when you cross a parrot with a zombie?

A A bird that talks your head off.

Q What do you get when you cross a spider with a parrot?

A A walkie-talkie.

A Fowl play.

Q How did the chicken get out of the egg?

A It hatched a plan.

Q What do you get when you cross a creeper with a chicken?

A Egg-splosions.

CHOCK-A-BLOCK

Building rule number one: don't get stuck between a block and a hard place.

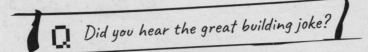

Q Did you hear the great building joke?

A Oh wait, it's not finished yet.

Q How does Steve party when he's finished building?

A He raises the roof.

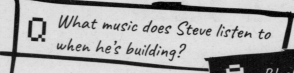

Q What music does Steve listen to when he's building?

A Block and roll.

I'd tell you the joke about the roof, but it'd probably go over your head.

Q Did you hear about the builder who built a village on a cliff?

A He liked living on the edge.

CREEPY CRAWLIES

Hopefully these jokes won't make your skin crawl ...

Q What are spider webs good for?

A Spiders.

Q What's worse than finding a spider in your base?

A Losing a spider in your base.

Q What do you get if you cross a spider and a chicken?

 **A** Webbed feet.

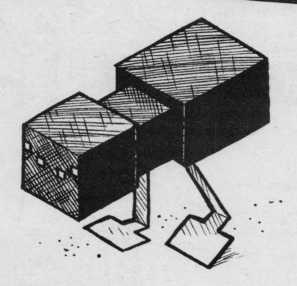

Q Why are spiders such a problem underground?

A Because they scare people out of their mines.

Q What do you get if you cross a cave spider with a cookie?

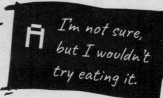

A I'm not sure, but I wouldn't try eating it.

ARACHNID ANTICS

These jokes could make you scream with laughter or terror!

Q *How did Steve know the spider was angry?*

A It was crawling up the wall.

Q Did you hear about the undercover arachnid?

A It was a spy-der.

Q Why did the spider buy a laptop?

A Because it wanted to build a website.

Q Why are spiders good swimmers?

A Because they have webbed feet.

Q *What do you get when you cross a creeper and a spider?*

A *A creepy crawly.*

TNT TITTERS

3, 2, 1 . . . get ready to blow your top with giggles.

Q Did you hear about the argument between the building and the TNT?

A It was blown out of proportion.

Q What did Alex say when she lost her TNT?

A Oh, blast.

Q What has four legs and goes BOOM?

A Two players fighting over a block of TNT.

Q Why are explosions in the rain depressing?

A It's all boom and gloom.

Q What do you get if you cross a clock with TNT?

A A ticking time bomb.

WIT AND WIZARDRY

Combine an enchantment with this book to magic up some laughs.

Q Which flower is like an enchantment?

A A rosebush, because it has thorns.

Q Which enchantment makes fish faster?

A Ef-fish-ciency.

Q Which enchantment hurts flying mobs?

A Ender-smite.

93

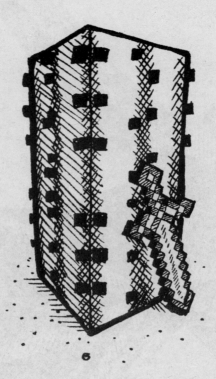

Q What's a cactus's favorite enchantment?

A Sharpness.

94

FLUFFY FUNNIES

They might both have fluffy white coats, but mix up the polar bear and the llama at your peril!

Steve: Did you see the animal film last night?

Alex: No, what did I miss?

Steve: Just some llama drama.

Q What did the llama say when it was told to leave the village?

A Alpaca my bags.

Q What do you call a polar bear in the desert?

A Lost.

Q How do you deal with a group of hostile llamas?

A You just have to get used to spit.

Q Why are polar bears bad at conversation?

A They're afraid to break the ice.

Q What do polar bears eat for lunch?

A Icebergers.

WITTY WITCHES
These jokes will really make you cackle!

Q What do you call a witch covered in sand?

Q Why did the witches stop being friends?

A A sand-witch.

A They were driving each other batty.

Q What do you call a witch that won't stop scratching?

A An itch.

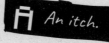

Q Why is it easy to confuse one witch with another?

A Because it's hard to tell which witch is which.

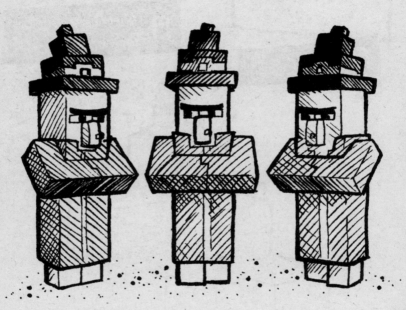

Q What do you call a witch in a hole?

A A ditch.

Q Why did the witch write a book?

A Because she was good at spelling.

FARMYARD FUNNIES

Have a giggle at these farmyard funnies.

Q Why do cows prefer the other side?

A Because the grass is always greener.

Q Did you hear about the giant cow in the tiny house?

A There wasn't mooshroom.

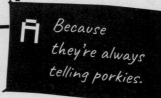

Q Why can't you trust a pig?

A Because they're always telling porkies.

Q What do you call a pig with three eyes?

A A piiig.

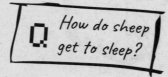

Q How do sheep get to sleep?

A They count themselves.

IN THE END

To get to these jokes, you'll need to find a chortle room.

Q What's the last block you should place when you finish a build?

A The End stone.

Q Why did Steve think the shulker was shy?

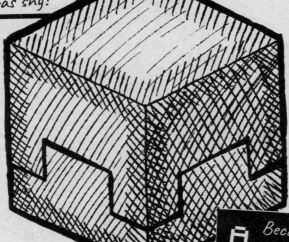

A Because it wouldn't come out of its shell.

Q What do you call an endermite that can't make up its mind?

A An ender-might.

Q Why do cats like End cities?

A Because they're made from purrpurr blocks.

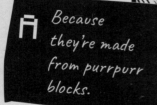

THE END OF THE END

Stop dragon your heels and read on!

Q Why are shulkers bad at telling jokes?

A Because they always start at the End.

Q Why do shulkers hide in their shells?

A Because they're shulking.

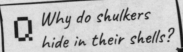

Q How many items can you put in an empty ender chest?

A One. Aftr one, it isn't empty anymore.

Q How did Steve feel when he defeated the ender dragon?

A Egg-cited.

Q What should you do when you're fed up with the End?

A You should a-void it.

MINE, ALL MINE!

Get back on track with this minecart full of cheer.

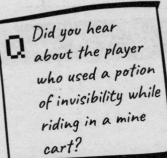

Q Did you hear about the player who used a potion of invisibility while riding in a mine cart?

A She was trying to cover her tracks.

Q Why was the mine cart so late?

A It really got off track.

Q How do you find a missing mine cart?

A Just follow the tracks.

Q Why was the mine cart late?

A It got sidetracked.

Steve: How many mine carts came off the rails?

Alex: I don't know, it's hard to keep track.

Q *Did you hear about the mine cart that lost control?*

A *It really went off the rails.*

PET PUNS

Wolf down these purrfect puns.

Q What did the skeleton say to the wolf?

A Bone-appétit.

Q What do you get if you cross a wolf with a sheep?

A A wolf in sheep's clothing.

Q What do you call a pile of kittens?

A A meowntain.

Q How do you know when a cat is hurt?

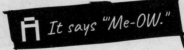

A It says "Me-OW."

Q What do you call
a messy cat?

A A shabby
tabby.

Q Why is it hard for ocelots to hide?

A Because they're
always spotted.

HALF-BAKED HUMOR

We hope these hot cross puns get a rise out of you.

Q What did Alex say to the tasty bread?

I loaf you.

A He was caught bread-handed.

Q When does bread rise?

A When you yeast expect it.

Q What did the angry cake say to Alex and Steve?

A You wanna piece of me?

Q Did you hear about the pumpkin pie that ran away?

A It desserted.

ENDERMANIA!

These jokes are a scream!

Q. Why don't endermen like jokes about water?

A. They only like dry humor.

Q. Where do endermen sleep?

A. Anywhere they like.

Q. Why are endermen so tall?

A. Because their feet smell.

Q *What do you call an enderman who has lost weight?*

A *A slenderman.*

Q *Why didn't the enderman cross the road?*

A *Because it teleported across instead.*

Q *What do you call an enderman that picks up TNT?*

A *Extremely dangerous.*

ALMOST AT THE END . . . ERMAN

These jokes will teleport you to the funny dimension.

Q What do you call a group of endermen?

A An enderclan.

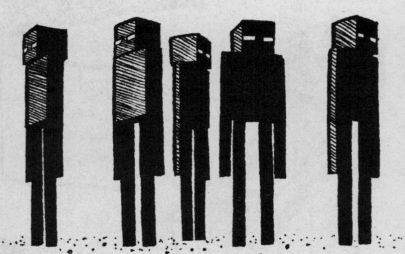

Q What do you get if you cross an enderman and a village priest?

A An end-amen.

Q What do you call it when Steve dresses up as an enderman?

A A pretenderman.

Q What do you call an enderman with feelings?

A A tenderman.

Q Why did the enderman live in a one-story house?

A Because it didn't like stares.

REPTILE ROARS

Read these jokes to make the ender dragon seem less scary!

Q What did the polite ender dragon say?

A Fang you very much.

Q Why are ender dragons bad at telling stories?

A They always drag on.

Q What does the ender dragon sound like?

A Roar-some.

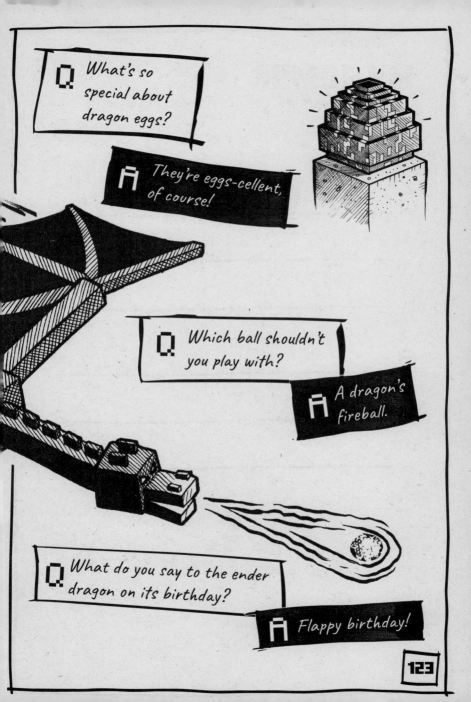

Q What's so special about dragon eggs?

A They're eggs-cellent, of course!

Q Which ball shouldn't you play with?

A A dragon's fireball.

Q What do you say to the ender dragon on its birthday?

A Flappy birthday!

MY HUMOR

Write your own Minecraft jokes, puns, and riddles!

Q _____

_____

_____

A _____

_____

_____

Q._____

_____

_____

A._____

_____

_____

_____